Welcome to "Life Skills for Little Ones"! In this book, you'll discover important life lessons that help you grow up happy, kind, and confident. From sharing with friends to being brave, each lesson teaches you something special about living a good life and making smart choices.

Explore these pages to learn how to be your best self, develop new skills, and spread joy.

Life Skills for Little Ones

Inspiring Lessons to Help Kids Grow, Learn, and Thrive

www.colorblastfilms.com

Published by Colorblast Films

First published 2024

© 2024 Colorblast Films

Growing Happy, Kind, and Confident

Being kind is cooler than being cool

"Treat everyone with respect"

You are unique
"Everyone is special in their own way."

Happiness comes from sharing with others

"Happiness grows when we share"

Take Your Time and Be Patient

"Good things happen when you wait patiently."

Pay Attention When Others Speak

"Listening to others shows kindness and respect."

A smile can brighten anyone's day

"Your smile can make someone's day better."

WE ALL MAKE MISTAKES

"It's okay to make mistakes; we learn from them."

TELL THE TRUTH

"Being honest helps everyone trust you."

HELP OTHERS

"HELPING OTHERS MAKES THE WORLD A BETTER PLACE."

LOVE YOUR FAMILY
"SHOWING LOVE TO YOUR FAMILY BRINGS EVERYONE CLOSER."

BE BRAVE

"COURAGE HELPS YOU HANDLE TOUGH SITUATIONS."

KEEP PROMISES

"Keeping promises shows you can be trusted."

Laugh Often

"Laughing makes you and others happy."

Apologize When You Hurt Someone
"Saying sorry helps heal hurt feelings."

DREAM BIG
"BIG DREAMS CAN LEAD TO AMAZING ADVENTURES."

STAY CURIOUS
"CURIOSITY LEADS TO AMAZING DISCOVERIES."

Learn Something New

"Learning new things every day makes you smart and happy."

Made in United States
Troutdale, OR
10/15/2024

23805911R00026